Murder on the Beach

Penelope Sotheby

Free Book

Sign up for this author's new release mailing list and receive a free copy of her very first novella _Murder At The Inn_. This fantastic whodunit will keep you guessing to the very end and is not currently available anywhere else.

Go to http://fantasticfiction.info/murder-at-the-inn/ to have a look.

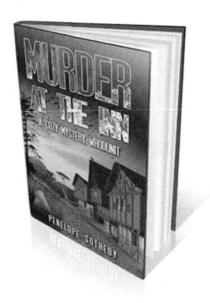

Other Books By The Author

Murder at the Inn

Murder on the Village Green (A Diane Dimbleby Cozy Mystery)

Murder in the Neighbourhood (A Diane Dimbleby Cozy Mystery)

Murder on a Yacht (A Diane Dimbleby Cozy Mystery)

Murder in the Village (A Diane Dimbleby Cozy Mystery)

Murder in the Mail (A Diane Dimbleby Cozy Mystery)

Murder in the Development (A Diane Dimbleby Cozy Mystery)

Murder in the Highlands (A Diane Dimbleby Cozy Mystery)

Table of Contents

Chapter 1

There was nothing quite like a spring morning on the quiet countryside of Apple Mews in Shropshire. Diane Dimbleby enjoyed taking her morning tea and breakfast outside to listen to the birds and watch the sun rise over the low mountains. From time to time, she would see a deer or rabbit scurrying along. Apple Mews had been Diane's home for most of her life. She was a teacher at the local school before meeting her husband David and moving to London. Her husband was a detective at Scotland Yard. They spent two gloriously happy years together in London before he was killed in the line of duty. After his death, she returned home to the only place she found real comfort at in the midst of tragedy.

Apple Mews was the type of town that went to bed early and woke up slowly. With less than a thousand residents in the quiet village, everyone knew everyone. And everyone knew everyone's business as well. Diane was no exception. She especially made it her point to know the goings on of Inspector Crothers, sometimes to his chagrin.

"Ms. Dimbleby, please remove yourself from my crime scene and let me do my job," the Inspector would say, right before she reminded him that on more than one occasion her input had helped him close a case. After retiring from teaching, she could not simply be one of those women who spent all of her time knitting, playing cards and watching the years tick by. Diane had always had a love for writing and now had the time to commit. Finally her own boss, she spent her afternoons leisurely writing and editing her novels, specifically crime novels. She enjoyed writing mysteries and found that life around her, even in Apple Mews, offered inspiration.

Unlike her quiet hometown, Diane could definitely do without the hustle and bustle of Plymouth in Devon, a much larger town home to hundreds of thousands of people. But her beloved nephew was getting married, and she could not miss it. Frederick Godwin had been the apple of Diane's eye since he was a small lad. Never having children of her own, she had doted on the boy from the day he was born. Frederick was her brother Martin's only son. He was a lawyer in Plymouth at the well-known firm Hanson and Gregory. It was there he met his soon-to-be wife, Emily. She was a lovely girl who also worked as an attorney.

"I knew from the moment I saw her that she would be my wife," Frederick had told his Aunt Diane. He was definitely smitten from the start, and after meeting Emily, Diane completely understood. The two complimented each other perfectly, Diane thought, as she put the finishing touches to her hair and makeup before making her way to the late afternoon wedding. She was staying at a quaint chalet close to the church where the wedding was being held. Well, as quaint as lodging could get in the city.

It was not family-owned and run like the hotel in Apple Mews, but the manager was friendly, the rooms were clean and stylish, and the breakfast had been delicious. She had chosen the location not just because of its proximity to the church, but also because it was near the beach. Diane loved to walk along the beach, feel the briny air and listen to the sounds of the ocean. On her first night, she had left her window slightly open in hopes of catching the sound of the waves lightly crashing against the sand. She was in luck that the chalet was just far enough from the major traffic that the only sounds she heard as she fell asleep were the waves.

Diane put a call in to her fiancé Albert who was back in Apple Mews looking after the dogs. He was meant to come along to the wedding also, but he twisted his ankle after falling over a rabbit hole and so was told to take it easy for a few days by the doctor. Diane thought that Albert fell deliberately to get out of what he deemed to be "a tedious bore" of a weekend. Just about anything that took Albert out of this beloved Apple Mews, was a tedious bore Diane thought. On the phone Albert told Diane that everything was fine and to stop fussing, before having to hang up as Strictly Come Dancing was coming on the television.

Diane noticed the time, silently scolded herself for being lost in thought, and gathered her things before hurrying out the door. The church had been decorated beautifully with hundreds of white, blue and yellow flowers, and the colors complimented the late spring weather. She remembered Frederick saying how concerned Emily was that unpredictable spring weather would mar their wedding day, but the day was perfect.

Diane signed the guestbook, noting the other guests attending the wedding, and was greeted by a young usher dressed in a suit that looked a bit too large for his frame.

"Good afternoon, ma'am," the young usher said. "Bride or groom?"

"Groom, please," she said. "Are you part of the bride's family?

"Yes, ma'am. The bride is my cousin," he said, beaming with pride. "Our mothers are sisters. She used to watch me when I was a boy."

"How lovely," Diane said, thinking that the young man was still quite a boy. She was escorted to the family area of the groom's side and caught sight of her brother's wife, Suzanne, who seemed to be running around with no clear place to go.

"The flowers look as if they are already wilting," Suzanne said to no one in particular. "And the time. The time is flittering away. The food will be cold by the time everyone gets to the reception."

"Everything is lovely, and the food will be fine," Martin said, catching up with his wife and pointing her back toward the pews to sit. On his way back, he caught sight of his sister. Diane gave him a wink and a smile, and he responded with a quick nod and eye-roll toward his wife.

Martin was Diane's younger brother by four years and her only sibling. Their parents had moved the family to Apple Mews when Diane and Martin were very young. Diane did not even remember living anywhere else. She had fallen in love with the small town as a child and, aside from college, had little intention of leaving before she met her husband. Martin, on the other hand, seemed eager to leave as soon as possible. He ended up in Devon, where he met his wife and started a family. Their parents had died only a few years after Martin finished college, and the siblings had made a point to see each other as often as possible. Life, as it does, continued to get busier as the years went by. Although they did not see one another as often as they would have liked, Diane and Martin always found the time.

The music began, and her nephew and his groomsmen took their places at the front of the church as the ushers escorted the remaining guests to their seats. A curly blonde-headed flower girl made her way down the aisle, dramatically tossing her basket of petals along the way. She was followed by a less than enthusiastic ring-bearer more interested in picking up the petals left behind than holding the little silk pillow and posing for pictures. Four bridesmaids followed dressed in slightly different but complimentary blue dresses, taking their place across from the best man. The maid of honor was Emily's sister, Marjorie, and the remaining bridesmaids were friends from college who had spent the entire week in Devon preparing for their friend's big day. Diane was reminded of the day she married David. Her two closest college girlfriends had traveled to Apple Mews to spend the days before her wedding getting everything, including the dress, ready.

After the bridesmaids had taken their places, the wedding march started. As Emily and her father made their way down the aisle, the guests stood with oooohs and ahhhhhs. The ceremony was beautiful, with the couple sharing their own personalized vows. After the "I dos," the wedding party and their guests were treated to a lovely outdoor reception and dance.

"Wonderful to see you, sweet sister," said her brother, Martin, kissing Diane on her cheek. "Very glad you could come."

"I would not miss it," she said. "Has the mother of the groom recovered?"

"Oh, you know Suzanne, only child and all," he answered. "And between the two of us, also a bit of a drama queen," he added quietly.

"I'll forget you said that," Diane said. "Even though I know exactly what you mean. I'm glad so many could come. It looks to be a successful day."

"Yes, yes. Did you see cousin Abbie?" he asked.

"No, where?" she asked.

"She's introducing yet another much younger man as her forever beau," her brother answered, motioning to an overweight, older woman staying close to the buffet. "And over there is Uncle Robbie. He specifically asked if you were coming, so you had better make an appearance. And I better go find Suzanne and make sure she isn't still inside the church trying to perk up the flowers."

Diane chuckled and watched him go. She scanned the crowd, recognizing a handful of old friends and family members. She and Martin did not have a very large extended family, but it appeared that everyone had made it to the wedding. Cousin Abbie caught her eye and rushed toward Diane. Abbie had been married three times that Diane knew of, and always seemed to be introducing someone new.

"Didi!" Abbie exclaimed. She was the only person in Diane's family who had ever called her Didi, and it was not something that Diane particularly liked then or now. But Abbie had been younger than Diane, and when she had tried to say her name, Didi was all that came out.

"Oh Abbie, I haven't gone by that name in years," she said. "I do prefer Diane."

"Of course, of course!" Abbie said. "Are you here with anyone? No? Well, I am, come meet him. He really is marvelous."

Abbie dragged Diane over to meet her companion, after which Diane mingled through the crowd, catching up with family she had not seen since moving back to Apple Mews several years earlier. The music began, and the crowd began to clap as Frederick and Emily entered the dance floor for their first dance. After the first song, the guests began to join in. Frederick saw his aunt and greeted her with a hardy hug.

"Aunt Diane!" he said. "I'm so glad you are here. Wasn't it beautiful? Wasn't she beautiful?"

"Oh yes, Freddie," she said. Diane was the only person who referred to Frederick as Freddie and was, in fact, the only person who could get away with it. "Everything was wonderful."

"Are you having fun?" he said. "Did you see mum and dad?"

"Of course I am," she said. "And yes, I saw both of them. Your mother seemed to take it well."

"Right," he chuckled. "How about Abbie and her new friend?"

"I could not have missed her if I tried, and I tried," Diane sighed.

Frederick smiled. "Come, I want to introduce you to some people," he said.

Frederick ushered his aunt through several people, introducing her to members of his new wife's family and some of his co-workers. "Oh, there he is," Frederick said, directing her toward a middle-aged man with salt-and-peppered hair standing next to Frederick's new father in law. "I really want you to meet Charles, I think the two of you would hit it off."

"This is Charles Godfrey, he is a friend of Emily's father," Frederick said, introducing her to the man. "Charles, this is my Aunt Diane. Charles is a Devon attorney, and Aunt Diane fancies herself a detective story writer."

Diane blushed as she shook Charles' hand and gave her nephew a disapproving glance.

"How fun and exciting," Charles said. "Sometimes I wish I could live a more interesting life in fiction."

"Now that's not true," Frederick said. "Charles is a very successful lawyer. He's tried several high-profile murder cases."

"Is that right?" Diane said excitedly. "I would love to pick your brain. After all, truth can be so much more compelling than fiction."

"There is truth to that I suppose," Charles replied. "I do think I could sit for a bit. Let's grab a drink, and you can pick away."

"And with that, I'll leave you two to it and go find my beautiful new wife for a dance," Frederick said, kissing his aunt on the cheek before disappearing through the crowd. Charles led Diane to the bar where they both chose a glass of white wine and found a quiet table toward the back of the reception.

"So do tell me what cases you have been involved in," Diane asked. "I thought your name sounded familiar, like I had seen it in the paper. Was it the triple murder in the Exeter underground? Or the murder/kidnapping in Torquay?"

"Both actually," Charles said, looking intrigued and surprised.

"Your firm represented the defendants, right?" Diane asked. "In the triple murder, is it true that the killer left behind drawings on the wall? And the kidnapping, is there really a tape no one has seen that clears the current suspect?"

Charles smiled broadly before letting out a small laugh. "I'm not sure if you are more insightful or imaginative," he said. "I cannot tell you everything I know, but I can tell you enough to satisfy the detective novelist in you."

Charles and Diane spent the rest of the evening discussing the prominent cases Charles had been and was involved in. Diane was excited to hear Charles' perspective, and she made hundreds of mental notes on taking the information he shared and expanding on some exciting fiction stories. Charles enjoyed hearing about Diane's crime-solving adventures in and around Apple Mews, and the love-hate relationship she shared with Inspector Crothers. Before they realized it, the evening had dwindled down to only a few remaining guests. Frederick and Emily had long since left the reception for their week-long honeymoon in Italy.

"Well, it has been a pleasure talking with you, but I'm afraid I must get some rest," she told Charles before gathering her coat and purse and saying her final goodbyes to the remaining family and friends. She made her way back to her chalet, readied herself for sleep and crawled into the comfortable bed, exhausted from the day. Despite the conversation topics of the evening, she slept soundly and happily.

Chapter 2

The morning sun broke through the curtains, waking Diane from her slumber. She was surprised she had slept as late as she had, but the previous evening had been tiring. Before checking in with Martin and Suzanne and heading back to Apple Mews, she decided a long walk along the beach next to her chalet was in order. Diane dressed in a light blue warm-up suit and tennis shoes before heading down to breakfast. She chose something light with her tea and headed off. The mid-morning air was refreshing, and the briny smell and crisp breeze coming off the ocean invigorated her walk.

Diane stepped onto the soft sand, looking at the seabirds. She walked toward the pier and walked along the wooden planks, listening to the soft creak and lapping water below her. A handful of people sat along the pier with fishing poles sitting lazily in the water.

"Good mornin' lady," a young boy aged no more than 10 said to her as she stepped up next to him. "Fine mornin' and the fish are bitin' still."

"Well good morning," she said smiling at him, looking at the small bunch of fish the boy had sitting next to him. "Looks like quite a haul."

The boy smiled back and her and picked up his fish. "Sure is," he said, scurrying away.

Diane walked back out to the beach and strolled along looking at the different shells across the sand. Out of the corner of her eye, she saw colorful movement. She looked up and noticed an open sun-umbrella rolling across the beach heading toward the water. The umbrella was a deep blue and looked rather expensive. Diane quickly looked around for its owner and, not seeing anyone, ran toward it. She caught up with it just before it rolled into the water. After shaking off the water and wet sand, Diane walked back over to where it appeared to have come from.

The weather was so nice that she expected to see others enjoying the morning on the beach and the owner of the umbrella, but there was no one in sight. She considered what to do with the umbrella, and decided to try and put it back where it appeared to have come from. Diane planted the umbrella as firmly as she could into the sand, wiped her hands across her trousers and continued her walk. She decided it would be nice to take off her socks and running shoes and put her feet in the water. Diane had bent down to do just that when she heard someone yelling from behind her. Diane turned and looked across the beach. She finally saw a man waving his arms somewhat wildly and hurrying in her direction.

"You there," the man yelled. "Hey, you there, lady. Stop."

Diane was sure she did not recognize the man and looked around again to see if perhaps he was talking to someone else. She still did not see anyone and considered ignoring him and continuing on her walk. After all, the man seemed upset, and she could not imagine why he would be yelling after her.

"Yes, ma'am, you there," he said pointing at her. "Stop. Wait."

Now convinced he was talking to her, Diane stopped and waited. She looked around again nervously, hoping to see anyone else around. The man hurried up to her and stopped, leaning over with his hands on his knees catching his breath. Diane waited a few moments, and the young man continued to breathe heavily.

"Are you okay?" she asked him. "Is there something I can help you with?"

The man stood up, finally able to take in a deep breath, and looked at Diane pointedly. "What are you doing?" he asked, someone angrily.

"What do you mean?" she asked.

"Why are you touching my things?" he asked.

"What things?" Diane said, confused.

"My umbrella!" the man said loudly. "Why did you run after my umbrella, take it and close it?"

Diane was very confused. She could not understand what this young man was saying. She had seen an unmanned umbrella rolling across an almost deserted beach heading toward the water and had done what anyone would have. She did not understand why he seemed so upset about it.

"The blue umbrella is yours?" she asked.

"Yes, of course it is," he said. "And I want to know why you picked it up."

"I did not see you, or anyone, so I put it back where I thought it came from," she said. "It's right there. I tried to plant it deeper into the sand so it would not blow away again."

"I can see that," the man said, still seemingly put out by Diane's actions, although she still could not understand why. "I can see that it is right there, but I'm asking you why you touched it in the first place."

"Well, I saw it rolling across the beach toward the water. It looked expensive, and I thought it was going to be ruined in the water. So I gallantly rescued it," she said, adding some humor to the idea of rescuing an umbrella. The man, however, was not amused. He picked up the umbrella, closed it and folded his arms across his chest.

"Listen, lady," he said curtly. "I did not ask you or anyone to touch my things. Please mind your own business and keep your hands off of things that do not belong to you."

With that, the man turned and hurried back across the beach, umbrella in hand. Diane stood, dumbfounded by the exchange. She watched the young man until he disappeared across the beach. She decided that her first thought of Plymouth was likely correct and that returning to Apple Mews was becoming more and more appealing. She turned toward her chalet and heading back intending to work on gathering her things and leaving this place, along with its rude, umbrella-crazed people behind.

Chapter 3

Diane tried to forget about her unfortunate encounter with the rude stranger on the beach and spent the rest of the afternoon taking in historic sites and touring lighthouses. She made reservations with a local touring company, which had a pick-up stop near the beach. There were dozens of lighthouses set along the English shore in Devon and Cornwall. Eddystone, or Smeaton's Tower, was her favorite. She marveled at the 250-year-old wonder and pictured early tradespeople wandering in the rough tide in rickety boats, finally setting eyes upon the light cast by the tower.

The sun began to set low in the sky and, tired from her afternoon, Diane decided to return to her chalet. She hopped the bus back to the beach near her room. She stopped in the lobby/kitchen area and picked out a sandwich, cookies, and tea before making her way up to her room. As she sat down at the small table in her room to unwrap her sandwich, she felt a cool breeze and saw movement out of the corner of her eye.

The window in her room that looked out toward the beach was open, and the curtain was fluttering in the evening breeze.

"Now I know I shut that," she said aloud to the empty room. "I know I did."

She put her sandwich down and walked across the room to the open window, eyeing it suspiciously. Everything was intact, including the panes and the latch. She moved the small brass hook up and down, not seeing any sign that the window was forced open.

Diane latched the window tightly and returned to her sandwich. She finished her meal, washed up for the evening and lay down with a book she had found in a used bookstore earlier in the day. Despite the riveting plot of her new book, her mind kept wandering back to the window. While logically she knew she must have shut the window before leaving, something about it kept nagging at her. Even after putting the book down and settling in, sleep did not come easily. She could not explain exactly why, but Diane felt that somehow her space had been invaded.

Chapter 4

Morning came much too quickly. Diane had not slept well and considered rolling over with a pillow over her head to catch a few more minutes of rest. She looked over at her laptop sitting on the small table in the room next to the remnants of the previous night's dinner and remembered that she had had not checked her emails in the past few days.

After washing her face and making a cup of tea, she powered up her small laptop and entered the Wi-Fi information provided by the hotel. The news began scrolling across her homepage, and something familiar caught her eye. Pictures of the man who had been so rude to her the day before on the beach were staring back at her under headlines touting "suspicious death" and "likely murder victim." Diane, a little shaky at the thought of someone she had just met being dead, clicked on the story and began reading. Apparently, the man was found dead on the beach from a fatal wound to his chest. Police were stating that while the first thought was that the man had died from a gunshot wound, preliminary reports were showing that his heart had been pierced with a small, cylindrical object. The news story also mentioned that blood evidence had also been found at the scene, including on the tip and fabric of a beach umbrella near the body.

At the mention of the beach umbrella, Diane's eyes widened, and her heart began to beat a little faster. She continued on and noticed that the only pictures included with the news story were two pictures of the victim and a picture of the beach. There did not appear to be any pictures of the actual crime scene, but Diane was certain that she knew where this had occurred. There was no description of the umbrella at the scene, other than the mention of blood, but Diane was certain that it must have been the very same umbrella she stopped from rolling into the ocean and replacing in the sand. It must have been the very same umbrella the now deceased young man had been so rude to Diane about.

While she had not dwelled on the reason for his strange behavior at the time, she certainly wondered about it now. Diane jumped from her seat, quickly dressing and readying herself for the day. She intended to find out what was so important to the man about that umbrella. So important, she thought, that it may have cost him his life.

After grabbing a quick breakfast on her way out of the chalet, Diane put on a hat and sunglasses and headed back to the beach. The area was much busier than it had been the previous day. She supposed that was because, in part at least, people may have been trying to get a look at what happened. As she approached the area, she noticed that an about thirty-foot area had been cordoned off with bright red and white police barricade tape. A small white tent was propped up where she had replaced the umbrella the previous day, and several small evidence tags were placed throughout the area around possible areas of interest. She tried to recall what had been there the previous day and remembered seeing a blue and yellow beach towel stretched out on the sand near where the white tent now stood. In fact, she was sure there had been a beach towel nearby because she thought the umbrella might have belonged to the same person who had put out the towel. Diane looked around for the towel. She had not wanted to get too close to the scene, so she had to crane her neck a bit. There was no sign of the towel, and she assumed it must have been swallowed up by the sea.

Turning on her heels to head back to the chalet, Diane noticed two people who appeared to be walking toward her. The lookie-loos who had been in the area earlier had all gone, and she was the only one left in that area of the beach. As it was a man and woman, she thought perhaps the pair was just strolling, but their clothes were not quite right for a beach walk. They also seemed to be intent on walking straight in her direction. Turning to look at the beach, Diane waited for the two strangers to walk past her. To her dismay, they did not. Instead, the pair stopped right in front of her.

"Good morning, ma'am," the woman said. "Can I ask what you are doing here?"

What an odd question, Diane thought. She began to speak, but paused, looking them up and down nervously. "Who are you?" she finally asked.

Both reached into their pockets and pulled out police badges. Diane studied them and realized that they were both detectives with the local police station She then realized that she probably should have figured this out from their clothing. The man was dressed in a light brown suit, matching loafers, and a plain white and brown tie. The woman was dressed very much the same, but her suit was dark blue with no tie.

"Now that we have that out of the way," the female detective said, "why don't you tell me what you are doing here so close to our crime scene?"

Diane knew there was no way around it, so she decided to explain everything she could as the detectives began writing in their notebooks.

"My name is Diane. Diane Dimbleby," she began. "I'm not from Devon, I'm actually from Apple Mews. I attended my nephew's wedding two days ago. I'm staying in a room at the chalet across the street. Yesterday, I thought it would be nice to take a stroll on the beach. I do love the beach."

Diane found herself speaking somewhat strangely and realized how nervous she actually was. Logically, she knew she had no real reason to be nervous as she had not done anything wrong. But speaking with the detectives about the death of a man she had encountered only the day before was unnerving her.

"Anyway, I started my stroll at the pier and continued along the beach close to the water," she said. "I had just decided to take off my socks and shoes for a little dip in the water when something caught my eye. I noticed a large blue and white beach umbrella rolling across the sand headed toward the water. It looked pricey, so I thought it best to catch and return it to the owner. I managed to grab it before the water caught it and put it back in the sand where I thought it had come from."

The two detectives gave each other a look that made Diane even more uncomfortable. "And then why did you decide to come back out here today and nose around the crime scene?" the male detective asked her.

"Oh, there's a little bit more to yesterday before today," she said.

"I see," the male detective said. "Go on."

"After I put the umbrella back in the sand ..." Diane began.

"Where did you put it?" the female detective asked her, cutting her narrative off.

"Well, I put it right over there where that white tent is set," she said.

"Interesting," the female detective said. "Go on."

"So I put the umbrella back in the sand and started off to finish my stroll," Diane said. "I heard a man yelling and turned to see someone coming toward me. I was not sure at first that the man wanted me, but he seemed to be speaking directly to me, so I waited."

"The man, did you know him?" the female detective asked.

"That's the thing," she said. "I did not know him. And he was very upset with me for touching his umbrella. I tried to explain that I was trying to keep it from being damaged, but he did not seem to care. He, in no uncertain terms, strictly told me to mind my own business and not touch his things. So this morning, when I saw that this man I had seen was murdered on the beach, I thought it best to come out here and see for myself."

The female detective finished her writing, flipped the notebook closed and looked intently at Diane.

"That's quite a story," the male detective said as he put his notebook away. "I can't imagine too many folks would return to where someone they had just met was murdered to have a look around." The female detective shot him a glance and looked kindly at Diane.

"Ms. Dimbleby, I'm Detective Hazel Donnelly," she said. "And this is my partner Detective Andrew Thorne. We are investigating the murder of the man you encountered on the beach. You may have some additional information we might need, and so I would like for you to come to the station with us."

"I believe I have told you everything that I know," Diane said, uncomfortable at the thought of being taken to a police station for questioning. "Couldn't I just give you my number to contact me?"

"As you have told us you are not from the area, I'm afraid that would not work," Detective Donnelly said. "I think it's best if we sort this out down at the station. We will also need to get your prints."

"My prints?" Diane asked.

"Yes," Detective Donnelly said. "You mentioned that you grabbed an umbrella. While I cannot say that it was the same umbrella, or that the umbrella was used as the murder weapon, it's enough for us to want your prints for comparison."

"I suppose I understand," Diane said. "Please let me grab my purse."

The detectives escorted Diane back to her room and allowed her to gather her purse and a jacket, as the station interview rooms had a tendency to get cold. She also saw her cell phone sitting near her laptop and scooped it up before leaving the room. She walked with them back toward the beach where Diane saw a plain white four-door hatchback among other cars in a visitor parking lot. Diane had seen unmarked police cars before, and although there was nothing to indicate the police, she was certain the hatchback belonged to her escorts. Detective Donnelly opened the back door of the white hatchback for Diane to get in, while her partner slid into the driver's seat. As they exited the parking lot and headed toward the police station, Diane had a sinking feeling as she recalled grabbing the umbrella. The detective attempted to draw Diane into some conversation about the events, but she had decided it might be best to be polite, but quiet.

Chapter 5

Detective Thorne pulled into a parking space at the back of the station, and both detectives got out of the car. The back two doors of the car did not open from the inside, so Diane had to wait until Detective Donnelly finished gathering her things before opening her door. She slowly stepped out and looked up at the station. It was a rather plain two-story, red-bricked building with a breezeway that attached to what Diane thought was a jail area. The detectives led her up some steps to a metal door. Donnelly leaned down and scanned a key card, and the door popped open with a short buzzing sound.

She was then escorted past a bullet-proof kiosk where intake deputies talked with visitors and shuffled paperwork around. There were several cubicles in the main area of the station behind the entrance, as well as a number of small rooms lining the hall. Police officers both in and out of uniform milled about. Donnelly and Thorne placed Diane in one of the rooms and asked her if she wanted anything.

"I would love a cup of tea and perhaps some water," Diane said.

"Sure thing," Detective Donnelly said. "Sit tight, we will be right back."

The door closed abruptly, and Diane felt herself shake a bit. She closed her eyes and took some deep breaths. It concerned her that it may have appeared to the detectives that Diane was acting suspiciously. Who was she kidding, she thought, she was acting suspiciously. If it was the same umbrella Diane had chased on the beach, they would likely find her fingerprints on it. The problem, she decided, was whether they would find any other fingerprints on the blasted thing. If yes, her story would certainly be considered plausible, and she would surely be left go to about her business. If no, Diane would not only be considered a suspect, she would likely jump to the top of the list of any suspects.

"What do you think?" Detective Thorne asked his partner as they stood on the opposite side of a one-way mirror looking into the room that held Diane Dimbleby.

"There's no evidence she knew the victim, and she certainly doesn't look like a murderer." Detective Donnelly said. "It just does not fit."

"There's no evidence she knew the victim yet," Detective Thorne corrected his partner. "And we have seen several murderers over the years that don't look like murderers. Remember the quiet librarian who killed the man who delivered her mail? I dare say she definitely did not look like a murderer."

"True," Donnelly said. "But the man who delivered the librarian's mail is also the same man who broke the librarian's heart when he returned to his wife. This is very different. I just don't see any motive here."

"Well, maybe we have not found it yet, or maybe there is not any," he said. "There certainly doesn't have to be for murder. She could just be an old bat who was mad at how the man talked to her, so she stabbed him with the umbrella."

Detective Donnelly nodded slowly, lost in thought. "Let's see what we find out from the fingerprints. Do you want to print her, or should I?"

"Oh, I definitely think you should," Throne replied. "She could be your grandmother. I'll get her tea."

Detective Thorne went toward the station's small kitchen with a smirk while his partner gathered an ink pad and print card.

Diane looked around the room before checking her watch. The detectives had left her alone in the room for at least 15 minutes, maybe more. She knew they were likely behind the large mirror in the room, but did not dare look their way. As the sobering thought of the entire situation started to occur to Diane, she realized there was only one option for her. The detectives had allowed her to keep her purse. She reached in and grabbed her cell phone and the business card she had been given at the wedding. She turned the business card over and looked at the personal cell phone that had been written on the back. After dialing the number, she put the phone up to her ear and waited for an answer. Four rings in, a deep male voice answered.

"Hello?" the voice said.

"Hello, Charles?" Diane said. "This is Diane Dimbleby. We met the other night at the wedding."

"Yes, Diane, of course, how are you?" he asked.

"Actually Charles, I'm in kind of a mess I think," she said. "I'm actually at the police station, in an interrogation room, and I believe I may be suspected of wrongdoing."

There was silence on the phone, and for a brief moment, Diane thought that either Charles had hung up on her or the call had been lost.

"Charles?" Diane asked.

"Yes, yes, I'm here," he said. "I'm just surprised by what you said. I cannot imagine that anyone would suspect you of any wrongdoing. What on earth do they think you have done?"

"I'm afraid they think I had something to do with a murder," she answered.

"A murder?" Charles asked, the shock apparent in his voice. "Are you pulling my leg? Is this some kind of joke?"

"I do wish it were a joke, but I am serious," she said. "I was hoping you might have a moment to possibly pop over to the police station."

Diane went on to give Charles a shortened version of the events that had occurred over the past two days, ending with her run-in with Detectives Thorne and Donnelly.

"Of course, of course," he said. "Give me 20 minutes. And Diane, do not talk to anyone or do anything without my presence. Do you understand?"

"Yes," Diane said gratefully. "And thank you."

Diane leaned back in the small metal chair in the interrogation room, a little relieved that Charles Godfrey had agreed to come to her rescue. She knew that he was a high-profile attorney and for him to take time out of his busy schedule to help a virtual stranger was a small miracle. The interrogation room door opened, and Detective Thorne came in with a small tray carrying the tea Diane had requested, along with honey, sugar and a stirring spoon. He placed the tray in front of her.

"Thank you," she said.

"Is there anything else I can get you to make you more comfortable?" he asked. Before Diane could answer, Detective Donnelly entered the room with a small metal basket. Inside the basket was a stack of thick, card stock paper, wipes and a long ink pad. The detective set the basket on the table in front of Diane.

"Here we are Ms. Dimbleby," Detective Donnelly said. "Let's get your fingerprints."

Diane hesitated, not sure whether her instructions from Charles Godfrey to not speak to anyone or do anything without him present extended to providing fingerprints. She decided that even if it did, providing her fingerprints was inevitable.

"Alright, here you are," she said, extending her hand to Detective Donnelly.

Chapter 6

Diane looked at her watch. It had been almost two hours since she had called Charles Godfrey. She did not think he would be able to see her as quickly as he had indicated, but she became more on edge as the minutes ticked by. Detective Donnelly had taken her fingerprints, letting her know that they had a print technician in the building who would be examining her prints immediately. Diane wondered what constituted immediately, concerned she may have to stay in the police station much longer than she wanted to. Actually, she decided, she had already been there much longer than she wanted to.

As she continued to wait, she felt as if the room was getting smaller. Diane realized that this was only her imagination, fueled by uncertainty and stress, but it did not dissuade her feeling. Finally, the door to the interrogation room opened, and Detectives Donnelly and Thom walked in with coffee, some Danishes, and a file folder. Diane was relieved to see the croissant and eagerly accepted it, as she had not eaten since the morning. They sat down across from her and put the file folder on the table. Detective Donnelly took a photo out of the folder and pushed it across to Diane. The photo was a smiling headshot of the young man Diane had encountered on the beach.

"Is this the man you met on the beach?" the detective asked.

"Yes. Yes, that is him," Diane answered.

"And you have stated you do not know the man, is that correct?" the detective said.

"That is correct," she answered. "I do not know him. Well, other than speaking with him on the beach yesterday. I had never met him before that. In fact, I would not even call that meeting him. We had such a short, terse conversation that it was only an encounter really. Who is he?"

"His name is Maxwell Carter," Detective Donnelly said. "Does that name ring any bells?"

Diane thought for a moment. "No, it doesn't," she said.

"You have also stated that you did not see him after your conversation on the beach, is that also correct?" Detective Donnelly said.

"Yes it is," Diane answered. "As I explained, I spent the rest of the day seeing sights and did not return to my room until almost dark."

"Diane, it is very important that you are honest with us," Detective Thom said. "Are you absolutely sure you did not know him a bit more than you are letting on?

Perhaps it was an accident. If you work with us now, we might be able to help you out."

Diane felt a surge of irritation bubbling to the top. She was more than happy to have a discussion about this situation, but it was clear that they were accusing her of a crime. And not just a crime, but murder. She looked pointedly at Detective Thom and decided that she would not give him the satisfaction of a response.

Detective Donnelly pulled another photo out of the file folder and passed it across to Diane. The photo showed the same blue and white umbrella that Diane had chased and picked up on the beach. There was blood on the tip of the umbrella, as well as spatter across the top.

"Our print technician managed it rather quickly," Detective Thom said. "Your prints were a match for prints found on this umbrella. We believe it to be the murder weapon. The fatal wound matches the pattern, but forensics will confirm."

"Well, that is to be expected, right?" Diane said. "I certainly would think my fingerprints would be on it. I did tell you that I handled the umbrella."

"Yes, you did," Detective Donnelly said. "The problem is, Diane, that your prints were the only ones on the umbrella."

That did not make sense, Diane thought. She absolutely expected her fingerprints to be on the umbrella, but she had not expected hers to be the only ones. The man who accosted her on the beach touched the umbrella as well. Or did he? It occurred to her that while she had taken the umbrella and planted it into the sand, she did not actually recall the man touching the umbrella in her presence. But surely he must have touched it at some point—he had made a very strong point that it was his umbrella. She tried to recall if the man was wearing gloves, but could not picture it. This was not making sense to her, and she was unsure how to explain it to the detectives.

"Well, um…" she began when the door burst open. Charles Godfrey, with an air of authority, was standing in the doorway to the interrogation room. He was dressed in a dark blue suit with a red tie and carried a small briefcase. Charles scanned the room and noted the coffee and small snacks on the table.

"Thank you for your courteousness detectives," he said. "And now I'd appreciate some privacy to talk to my client."

"Your client?" Detective Thom said.

"Yes, my client," Godfrey said.

"Is this what you want, Diane?" Detective Donnelly asked. "You want to talk to us through a lawyer?"

"I don't really know what is happening here, and everything is moving rather fast," Diane replied. "I think that it is best for me to take a step back and speak with someone outside of the police force. So yes, I want to talk to my lawyer before proceeding."

The detectives gathered their things and began to exit the interrogation room.

"And detectives," Godfrey said. "Let's make sure that the one-way mirror is just a mirror."

Detective Donnelly nodded, while her partner smirked. They left the room, leaving Diane and Charles Godfrey alone to discuss the situation.

Chapter 7

"Thank you so much, Charles," Diane said, her voice starting quaver. She had not realized how close she was to tears until he had appeared. "I did not know who else to call."

"You did the right thing," he said, opening his briefcase and taking out a pen and notepad. "How are you holding up?"

Diane considered this question. It seemed everything really was moving so quickly, and she did not know how she felt. Only a few hours earlier, she was standing on the beach next to a crime scene trying to be helpful. She realized how it must have looked to someone who did not know her, but it was important that everyone understood she had nothing to do with this murder and was only trying to help. Diane took a deep breath, realizing that she was really only in a room answering some questions, and now that Charles was here, things would get worked out. She decided she felt silly for tearing up a bit.

"I'm holding up well, thank you for asking," she said. "Now that you are here, I am sure everything is going to be just fine."

"I'm sure," he said. "Now tell me everything about what has happened from the time you left the wedding that led you to this room being questioned by a detective about a murder."

Diane began telling Charles what she had done and endured over the past two days. She started with her decision to take a stroll on the beach the morning after the wedding, her walk along the pier where she saw locals fishing and her chat with the young boy.

"He was quite a funny lad and had a string of fish already," she said. "I suspect he spends a lot of time on that pier and not where he is supposed to be."

She continued telling Charles about her time on the beach and described seeing the blue and white umbrella rolling across the sand toward the water. She explained how she ran after it, grabbed it by the handle before it became wet and planted it back in the sand near a towel where she thought the umbrella had originally been.

"Did the detectives tell you the murder weapon was the same umbrella you handled on the beach?" he asked. Diane nodded. Charles looked down at Diane's hands and noticed the remnants of black fingerprint ink.

"It looks like they printed you," he said. "How long ago?"

"It was shortly after I arrived," she said.

"Was this before or after we spoke?" he asked.

"After," Diane said sheepishly, remembering Charles' instructions not to say or do anything.

"Well, no matter now," he said. "I'd be surprised if anything came back yet."

"Actually, one of the detectives said they had a fingerprint technician on hand, and they have already had something back," Diane said. "My fingerprints were on the umbrella."

"Nothing to worry about," Charles said. "You've already said what happened. It helps your story, as your fingerprints should be on there."

"The thing is," Diane said. "My fingerprints were apparently the only ones on the umbrella."

Charles looked up abruptly from his note taking. "Well that is bizarre," he said.

"I thought that as well, then something occurred to me," she said. "Of course my prints would be on it, and I certainly expected the young man's to be on it as well. But I do not actually recall him touching the umbrella, at least not in my presence."

Diane went on to tell Charles about the awkward encounter with the young man on the beach, how he had yelled at her and accosted her for touching his umbrella.

"He actually told me to mind my own business and keep my hands off of his things," she said, becoming flustered at the memory of it all. "I mean, the nerve of him, after I really was only trying to do the right thing. But he did not actually take the umbrella from me. We did not speak until after I had already placed it in the sand."

Charles continued taking notes, nodding at times. Diane went on to tell him about her return to her room, waking up the next morning and finding a picture of the man she had seen the previous day on the news. She explained that she felt it necessary to return to the beach and see if she could locate anything of interest that might be helpful.

"As I was leaving, the detectives noticed me and inquired as to what I was doing," she said. "I decided I must be honest with them, and the next thing I knew I was in this room being questioned and fingerprinted."

"Is there anything else you can tell me?" Charles asked.

"The detectives told me the young man's name was Maxwell Carter," she said. "Do you know who that is?"

"I don't believe so," Charles answered. "I take it you did not recognize the name either."

"No, I do not," she said. "He certainly did not tell me his name while he was berating me for touching his umbrella."

Charles closed up his notebook, took off his glasses and put both items into his briefcase. He appeared to be thinking through what he wanted to say next, and this made Diane somewhat concerned.

"I think there is more information out there to discover," he said. "They do not have enough to hold you any further on, and I am going to insist you be returned to your hotel. I want you to get something to eat, get some rest and wait for me to call you in the morning."

Diane agreed and thanked Charles again. "Wait here while I talk to the detectives about taking you back," he said.

Charles gathered his things and left the room. Detective Thom was waiting outside of the room, leaning against a vacant wooden desk while sipping on a cup of coffee. He was also holding a file folder. He opened the folder and motioned Charles to join him.

"Detective Thom," Charles said. "I am going to have to insist that you take Mrs. Dimbleby back to her chalet. There is not enough evidence to keep her in that room, much less arrest her."

The detective looked at Charles and nodded. He held up the report he was looking at and said, "I think I am going to have to agree with you. This is the autopsy report."

Detective Thom pulled away from the desk he had been leaning on and walked over to Charles. He gave him the report and allowed him a few minutes to review it. The detective pointed out that Maxwell Carter's wound was made by piercing his sternum with the tip of the umbrella.

"Diane Dimbleby is a slight woman," the detective said. "She can't be too much over five foot. The victim, in this case, was a strong, athletic man who jogged and did weight training regularly. It just doesn't seem likely that she had the strength to pierce an umbrella through Maxwell Carter's sternum."

"So you have settled on the umbrella as the murder weapon?" Charles said.

"Yes," the detective said. "The blood type found on the umbrella is a match to Maxwell Carter, and the wound is a match to the tip of the umbrella. The umbrella is simply not sharp enough to penetrate without significant force, and that is something Diane Dimbleby is not capable of providing."

"Well then that settles it," Charles said. "When will you be taking Diane back to her chalet?"

"We will take her back shortly," Detective Thom said. "But even with this report, it does not mean she was not involved in some capacity. We will need to interview her again, so she will need to stick around Plymouth for a bit longer."

"Shortly is not a sufficient answer," Charles said. "How about I take her back?"

"That's not going to work for me," Detective Thom said. "You see, I want to make sure I know exactly where she is staying, who the proprietor is and how I can get a hold of her when I need to."

"I'm afraid I must insist that I accompany you in getting her back to her room quickly and safely," Charles said.

"Suit yourself," the detective said. "Give me five minutes, and I will drive her back. You are welcome to follow."

Chapter 8

Detective Thom escorted Diane from the interrogation room, allowing her to stop off at the ladies' room, to the same unmarked car she had arrived at the police station in. Charles was waiting near the car as soon as they exited the building. He explained to Diane that the detective felt it necessary to escort her back to her room and why.

"That's ridiculous," she said, ensuring the detective could hear her.

"I agree," Charles said. "But it is what it is, and I am going to follow along and make sure you get back to where you need to be."

The detective opened the back car door for Diane, and once again she crawled into the back seat, still feeling like a suspected criminal. She would have much rather Charles drove her back in his car. At least then she could have sat in the front seat like a normal passenger. They rode in silence all the way back to her chalet. Detective Thom pulled the unmarked police car into the small parking area closest to the entrance, and Charles Godfrey pulled in next to the side Diane was sitting. He got out of his silver Mercedes-Benz and looked warmly at Diane through the window. The detective opened the door, and she stepped out of the car and walked toward the entrance. As she reached for the door handle, she stopped and turned to Detective Thom.

"Now I have given you my contact information, my time and my patience," she said. "Mr. Godfrey also has all of my contact information, and if you bother to look you will see there is nothing in my background that could possibly make you think that I will not be cooperative in every way possible. So, if you don't mind, there is no reason for you to accompany me any further."

Detective Thom thought for a moment, looking at Charles Godfrey who had a slight smirk teasing the corners of his mouth. He opted to agree, for the moment at least, with Diane and left her to continue into the hotel without him. Any information he could need on the proprietor or any of the guests could be done easily enough by phone. The detective gave a quick nod, returned to his car and left.

"I see you can take care of yourself very well," Charles said. "Even so, if you do not mind, I think I will walk you the rest of the way in."

Diane agreed, and they both headed toward her room. She made two cups of hot tea, and they sat down at the small table in the room. After the day she had endured, Diane could not help but feel a great sense of comfort and release as she relaxed in her room. She again heard the sound of the ocean outside and looked toward her window. It was as she had left it, but the uneasy feeling from finding it open before struck her again. She decided to tell Charles about the open window in her room, and the uneasy feeling she had.

"I'm sure I could have left it open," she said. "But I just do not remember doing so, and I typically close and lock any window or door before leaving a room with my belongings in it."

"Did you tell the detectives about this?" he asked

Diane shook her head. She contemplated why she had not mentioned it to the detectives and decided that it would have sounded made up in the middle of her questioning like she was trying to deflect.

"No," she said. "Things were so topsy-turvy today that I did not think it was the appropriate time to mention it. Perhaps I should have. Mentioning it now might sound even stranger."

"I will take care of it," Charles said.

After Charles had left, Diane went back down to the food service area and picked a sandwich and a bag of crisps out for dinner. A stack of local newspapers was sitting in the lobby by the food cart, and she saw Maxwell Carter's picture looking back at her. She picked up a copy. She ate her dinner in her room and read the paper. The reporter had quoted Detective Donnelly, making

Diane curious about finding out a little more on both detectives. She cleaned up after her meal, pulled out her laptop and started searching for information.

Diane started with the police station website, which only provided the names, ranks and precinct locations of members of the force. She used a few search engines, entering their names and the limited information she had gleaned from meeting them. There was not much to be found on Detective Thom, except for one picture of him with a group of new officers several years earlier. However, Diane was surprised on what she discovered about Detective Donnelly. Hazel Donnelly apparently had a previous career in modeling. Diane found several photos from a modeling website of the detective posing in different revealing outfits, including one rather skimpy red bikini. The pictures were professionally done, and Diane thought that they were likely taken for a catalogue or a magazine. She studied the images looking for a photographer credit, but there was nothing on any of the photos to indicate who took them.

"Interesting," Diane said aloud to her empty room. "I would never have guessed it."

Exhausted from the day, she decided her virtual sleuthing was over for the night. She turned off and put away her computer and considered taking a long, hot bath to relax. Diane decided she was even too tired for that. After finishing her nightly rituals, she lay down on the soft pillow and quickly became groggy. Her last thought before sleep overcame her was what could possibly be in store for her tomorrow.

Chapter 9

Diane was restless the entire night after her ordeal at the police station. When she was able to sleep, she dreamt of a stranger standing at her window trying to get in. This thought interrupted her sleep even more. When the sun began peeking through the smattering of clouds, Diane finally decided to give up on any further restful sleep and start the day. She took her time showering and getting ready, thinking about what she could do to take her mind off of the events of the past few days. A little forced retail therapy was in order, she decided.

Although she had taken the touring bus the previous day, Diane thought that since it was apparent she would be staying in town longer than expected, it was best if she drove herself to get some shopping done. She did not own a car but utilized a hire car when needed. There was only one place in Apple Mews that rented, and the selection was small. She had picked out a four-door, reasonably priced hire car to bring her to Devon.

Before leaving the chalet, Diane's cell phone rang. She looked down and saw it was her brother.

"Hello Martin," she said, remembering that she had forgotten to let her brother know she would be staying in town. "Did the newlyweds make it off okay?"

"Yes, off and having a marvelous time I have no doubt," he said. "I was starting to get a little worried about you, though. I thought you were going to call me when you made it back to Apple Mews."

Diane had completely forgotten to let her brother know that she would be spending an extra few days in Devon. She had not wanted to bring him into the sordid mess now consuming her trip but felt she must offer some sort of explanation.

"Oh, Martin, I am so sorry," she said. "At the last minute, I decided to stay a few extra days and forgot to let you know. I wanted to get a little shopping in and see some of the lighthouses."

"Just glad to know you're safe," he said. "Since you are still in Plymouth, Suzanne will insist you stop by for dinner before you head home."

"That sounds lovely," she said, trying to sound as convincing as possible. "I'll give you a ring."

Diane hung up and then phoned Albert. She decided not to tell him the whole story either at this point as there was nothing he could do and he would just worry. Diane told him that she decided to spend a few more days down in Plymouth to do some research for her next book. As this was a typical thing that Diane would do,

Albert had no reason to doubt her and he seemed satisfied as she ended the call.

Diane put the phone back in her bag and headed to her hire car. She struggled a bit with opening the door, something she had noticed since arriving in Plymouth. After checking the small map on her phone, Diane drove to the closest shopping center. It was the middle of the day midweek, and the streets and shopping area were not too crowded. It looked like there were several quaint clothing and antique shops in the area that Diane would have enjoyed, but she decided a bit of grocery shopping should be done first. She opened the car door, again with a little trouble, and walked toward the market. As the automatic door opened in front of her, Diane felt a lump catch in her throat when she saw Maxwell Carter staring back at her from the window of the electronics store next door. She slowly stepped away from the grocery store and found herself in front of the electronics store window studying a photograph of Maxwell Carter. Below the photograph was a small biography on a white card bordered slightly in black. She leaned in and read.

Maxwell Carter—Local famed photographer Maxwell Carter's latest exhibit The Eyes in Walls can be seen at The Art's Center in Devon. Carter is a self-taught artist who specializes in the use of light and shadow to add texture to pieces from everyday objects to the human form. Carter's artistic inspiration comes from photographers Lie Friedlander and Andres Serrano.

Interesting, Diane thought. She made a mental note to stop by the gallery and to see the photos as she turned to go into the grocery store. She took a small basket from the front of the store, put her bag in the front and gathered a few necessities to last her through the week. She also picked up a small container of lubricant spray, thinking it would help with the sticky door on the car. She checked out and led the young man who bagged her items to the car.

"Do you go to the electronics store often?" she asked him as he put the bag in the trunk of the hire car.

"Yes, ma'am," he answered. "I stop in a few times a week to trade out games. Why do you ask?"

"The poster in the window there of the photographer—have you noticed how long it has been up there?" she asked.

"A week or so I think," he said. "Not too long. There used to be a movie poster. I remember that because I had asked if I could have the poster when they were done with it."

"Did you get the poster?" she asked.

"Oh, I wish," he said. "Someone had beat me to it."

Diane thanked the young man and turned to get into the car when she again struggled with the door. Before she could try out the spray she had just purchased, the young man saw her struggle and assisted her with opening the door.

"Wow, that is a bit sticky," he said, also struggling with the door. "Ah, got it."

"Thank you so much," she said. Diane was beginning to think that car doors were becoming somewhat of an issue for her as she aged and was glad to see someone else struggle with the door. A few minutes later she pulled into the small parking area next to her chalet. She opened the trunk, attempting to carry all of the bags to avoid multiple trips, but leaving the spray in the car. As she neared the door, a woman got out of a small red car and began hurrying over to Diane. The woman was wearing black stretch trousers, a long, crisp white shirt and camel-colored boots that came up to the bottom of her knees. Her long black hair was pulled into a bun, and she had on large sunglasses and deep, red lipstick. The woman also carried a red bag that matched her shade of lipstick to a tee.

"Do you need some help?" the woman asked Diane.

After her recent interactions with strangers—the man on the beach and the detectives—Diane was a little skeptical about talking to, much less taking assistance from, anyone she did not know.

"No thank you," Diane said. "I believe I have it."

"I don't mind, and I need to speak with you," the woman said, taking off her sunglasses.

"Do I know you?" Diane asked.

"No, you do not," the woman said. "I need to know if you found a camera on the beach."

"Why would you be asking me this?" Diane said, putting her groceries down next to her and reaching into her bag to find her cell phone. This woman was making her uncomfortable. She was not sure if this was another police officer or a reporter, but Diane wanted to make sure she had quick access to Charles if need be.

"Look, I know that you were with Maxwell two days ago on the beach, and I know that you were messing with his umbrella," the woman said. "I need to know if you found a camera there or even any camera equipment."

"Who are you?" Diane demanded.

"My name is Angela," she said. "I was Maxwell's girlfriend."

Angela put her head down in her hands and began to cry softly. Diane pulled her hand out of her bag and gently patted Angela on the shoulder.

"I'm sorry," Angela said. "I shouldn't be blubbering to you."

"That's alright dear," Diane said. "I am sorry for your loss, but I did not see a camera. My interaction with Maxwell was brief and terse. Were there special photos on the camera that you are wanting to remember him by?"

"Not exactly," Angela said, dabbing the corner of her eyes. "Couples sometimes like to throw a little spice into the relationship. We did this by Maxwell taking some rather compromising pictures of me. It was shortly before his trip to the beach. I really need the memory card out of the camera to delete the pictures. I would be devastated if the pictures were to surface."

Diane thought this a bit strange. She would think that Angela would be devastated over losing a man she loved, assuming she loved him, but she seemed to be more worried about the photos. It was certainly not Diane's place to judge, however, as she had no idea how compromising the pictures were.

"Are you sure you did not see a camera or perhaps pick something up?" Angela asked. "The memory card could have been left behind even without the camera."

"Look, I am not sure how you found out about my interaction with Maxwell, but I did not know him," Diane said pointedly. "I would have had no reason to pick anything up."

"You did pick up his umbrella," Angela said.

Diane was getting very tired of telling the same story over and over again to random strangers who seemed to know a lot more about what was going on than she did.

"I was trying to keep it from being damaged," she said. "I did not know who he was until I saw his picture earlier today in an electronic shop near the grocery store. I have no idea why he was so upset about me touching his umbrella, but that really was all there was to it."

Angela nodded, putting her sunglasses back on her face and fishing her keys out of the red purse she was carrying.

"I understand," she said, her voice cracking with emotion. "I am sorry to be a bother."

Diane felt a little guilty. After all, the woman had just lost her boyfriend and was facing some embarrassment with the possibility of the photos she mentioned being discovered. She tried to end the conversation on a gentler note.

"You're not a bother," she said. "I apologize for my tone. It has been somewhat stressful since my interaction with Maxwell, but that is certainly no reason to be rude to someone who has just had a loss such as yours."

"Thank you, Diane. Let's do keep in touch about this shall we?" Angela said, pulling a card from her purse and handing it to Diane. "You are such a doll."

Angela hurried back to her car, and Diane picked up her grocery bags and headed for her room. She shook her head at yet another peculiar interaction with a complete stranger. She hoped she would not see Angela again, mainly because she really had nothing else to add to what she had already told her. After putting up her food, she decided to go to the gallery featuring Maxwell Carter's photographs.

Chapter 10

The Arts Center was not too far from her hotel and was closer than the market she visited earlier. Diane decided a short walk would be good for her and covered the five blocks in about twenty minutes. She walked into the gallery and noticed several different exhibits that caught her eye. She likely could have stayed the afternoon, but had other things to accomplish and headed straight for the photography exhibit.

Diane did not consider herself much of an art critic. As with most people, she knew what she liked, but also understood that attraction to art was subjective. Maxwell Carter's exhibit was not what she particularly liked. There were several photos Diane thought she might have been able to take herself, although maybe not with the same perspective. There were photos of several inanimate objects, like a chair, a chair with a table, a watering can and wooden blocks in different shapes.

"Really?" she said a little louder than intended.

"Aren't they marvelous?" a short man in a three-piece suit said as he approached her. The man was wearing round, wire-rimmed spectacles and had fashioned the remainder of his brown hair across the top of his head. "They really speak, don't they?"

Not wanting to be rude, Diane just smiled and nodded.

"Did you know the artist?" Diane asked.

"Of course," the man said. "He was one of a kind."

Right, Diane thought. If these pictures were one of a kind, she was the Queen of Sheba. The man looked Diane up and down, frowned slightly and excused himself. He likely was looking for a sale of these one-of-a-kind photos and noticed other patrons more likely to spend their money.

Diane started to leave unimpressed when she noticed some additional photos in a separate room that were part of the exhibit. These photos were definitely not of inanimate objects. These objects were quite animated, as well as scantily dressed. Diane felt herself blushing and began to turn away when she noticed a familiar face in the photos. She drew closer to the photograph and studied it. She was sure that a young Hazel Donnelly was staring back at her. Diane recalled the photos she found on the internet and wondered if Maxwell had taken them. She also wondered if Detective Donnelly had been in some kind of prior relationship with Maxwell when the two were younger. If that was the case, perhaps Detective Donnelly should not be involved in investigating his murder.

Chapter 11

After returning to her room and having a quick lunch, Diane decided to spend some time doing what she loved—writing. She opened up her laptop and delved back into her most recent novel. Writing well involved closing her mind to the outside world and stepping into the world she was creating in her imagination. This was one of the reasons she loved living in Apple Mews and felt a sudden sense of longing for home. She decided she was just going to have to find a way to make it work here in Devon. Diane spent several hours writing, looking up only when her stomach began to grumble.

She saved her work, put the laptop away and thought about what sounded good for dinner. Pasta, she decided, and headed toward the small kitchenette. She had just started to fill a pot with water and wash some fresh tomatoes when she heard a knock at the door. Looking out the peephole she let out an audible sigh of frustration when she saw Detectives Thom and Donnelly standing outside her door. Diane opened the door and greeted them.

"Good evening, detectives," she said. "I was not expecting to see you so soon. Please come in. Can I get you something to drink? Coffee, perhaps?"

"No, thank you," Detective Donnelly said. "We are fine. We just need to talk a bit more."

"I feel like I have told you absolutely everything I know," Diane said.

"Perhaps, but we have some follow-up questions," Detective Donnelly said. "Did you know Maxwell Carter was a photographer?"

"As I have told you that I did not know the man, then surely you would understand that I would have had no knowledge of what his occupation or hobbies are," Diane said, sounding more than frustrated.

"So that is a no," Detective Thom said.

"No, I did not know he was a photographer when I first encountered him," Diane said. "I did, however, find out today when I went to the market. There was a photograph of him with a short biography under it stating he was a photographer and had a local exhibit."

"We are looking for something related to his profession as a photographer that might give some insight into his death," Detective Donnelly said. "Do you mind if we look around your room and your car?"

"What exactly are you looking for?" Diane asked, suspecting she already knew what the answer would be.

"His camera or the memory card from it," Detective Thom said. "Both are missing. We believe there may be some pictures that may point to who killed him."

"And what makes you think that it would be in my possession?" Diane asked.

"You were the last known person to see him alive," he said. "We are just covering all our bases."

Diane took a deep breath before responding. "Detectives, you have already covered all of your bases with me," she said. "You know that I could not have killed Maxwell Carter, and I have explained ad nauseam that I did not know the man. Perhaps if you are looking for someone who might have actual knowledge of where he keeps his camera equipment, you should talk to his girlfriend, Angela."

The detectives looked at one another, a puzzled looked on each of their faces.

"How do you know that Maxwell Carter had a girlfriend named Angela?" Detective Donnelly asked.

"Because I have met her," Diane said. "In fact, I met her only today."

Diane recounted the events of the afternoon to the detectives, explaining that she had been approached by Angela when she returned from the store. She explained how interested Angela was in finding the camera or memory card due to some compromising pictures that Maxwell had taken of her.

"She seemed very upset about the photos," Diane said.

"Why would she think that you had them?" Detective Donnelly asked.

"I suppose because she knew I interacted with him on the beach," Diane said. "Although I am not sure how she knew. In fact, I find it extremely odd that not only did she know about what happened, but where I was staying. I don't suppose that either of you told her about me, did you?"

"No ma'am," Detective Thom said. "We do not comment to civilians on pending investigations. Did she say anything else?

"She did not. Now, I would be happy to let you search my home away from home here, and my car," she said. "But not without a warrant."

The detectives frowned as they put away their notebooks and stood to leave.

"Are you sure this is how you want to play it, Diane?" Detective Donnelly asked.

"Oh yes, that is exactly what I would like to do," Diane said. "I believe my life and liberties have been intruded upon enough during my short time here in Devon. There has been someone in the room going through my things already, and it's not going to happen again without a warrant."

Diane followed the detectives to the door and, before they left, questioned Detective Donnelly about the photographs of her she had seen earlier.

"By the way, Detective Donnelly, did you know Maxwell Carter?" Diane asked.

Detective Donnelly seemed somewhat surprised by the question and took a moment too long to reply.

"Yes I did," she said. "Although I did not know him very well, I had met him before. Anyway, I'll have you remember that it is not your place to ask the police questions. That is our job."

"It's a bit strange that you did not know him well," Diane said, with a small smile she could not stop appearing at the corner of her lips. "After I saw the picture of Maxwell in the electronics store, I decided to go and view some of his photography. I noticed a picture of you in his exhibit. It was a young and barely clothed Hazel Donnelly, but it was definitely you."

Diane's comments obviously flustered the detective, and she quickly looked down to hide her embarrassment. It appeared she was going to make some reply, but instead she left quietly and quickly with Detective Thom following behind her. Diane shut and locked the door and returned to fixing her dinner. She boiled the pasta, cooked down the tomatoes in some garlic and olive oil and tossed everything together with a bit of parmesan. When Diane was finally able to sit down to eat, she found that she was not as hungry as she had been before the detectives came.

Chapter 12

After cleaning up the kitchenette and putting away the leftover pasta, Diane sat down in front of her laptop to do a little more writing on her novel. Inside was feeling a little stuffy, so she decided to open the window for some fresh air. As her hand reached out to open the latch, a troubling thought occurred to her. Diane was certain that she had closed the window before her day on the beach when she encountered Maxwell Carter and his umbrella. She could not shake the feeling that someone had been in her room sometime that day or evening before she returned. Diane had assumed that if someone was in her room, it was because they were looking for something to take out of it. A panic began to envelop her as she considered the possibility that the person or people could have been leaving something instead. Someone could be trying to frame her for Maxwell Carter's murder. Her mind immediately went to the memory card.

"How would I even begin to find the bloody thing?" she wondered aloud. A memory card would be small enough to hide almost anywhere. Then she remembered something that might be able to help her. In a recent novel, one of Diane's characters was looking for a piece of jewelry and used a vacuum, piece of string and a scarf to search her car. If this memory card was in her room, that might be just the way to find it. She commandeered a vacuum cleaner from a closet in the lobby area, pulled a stocking out of her suitcase and used a rubber band to secure the stocking to the end of the hose. She turned on the vacuum and began to slowly and methodically search every space in her room. She started with the bedroom area, pushing the hose far underneath the bed and running it along the baseboards. She ran the stocking-sealed hose through drawers, in cabinets and behind furniture and appliances. After about 20 minutes of searching, Diane had found dust bunnies, loose change and small pieces of paper, but no memory card. She began to wonder if perhaps she was overreacting until she shoved the hose between the couch cushions and something caught.

Diane pulled the hose out, expecting a coin, when she saw a small black plastic rectangle. She pulled it off and saw that it was a digital camera memory card. She stared at the card, a sense of unease flowing through her as she realized that someone really had invaded her privacy. She turned the vacuum off and let the memory card fall to the top of one of the couch cushions. Looking at the card made Diane very nervous, and considering her previous treatment by the detectives, her first instinct was to get rid of it. Diane grabbed a paper towel, picked up the card and hurried outside. She looked around the garden area until she found a flat rock. Diane pried up the rock, wrapped the memory card in the paper towel to protect it and placed it under the rock. After replacing the rock, she patted the dirt back around the rock to disguise that it had been moved. When she returned to her room, she took the vacuum back to the hall closet and readied herself for bed. Before laying down, she double checked the latches on all the windows and the lock on the door.

Chapter 13

Shortly after Diane finished her breakfast the next morning, there came a brisk knock at the door. She looked through the peephole and again found Detectives Thom and Donnelly standing outside. As she invited the detectives in, they showed her a warrant to search the premises. Diane took the warrant and reviewed it, noting the language referred to evidence related to or used in the commission of a criminal offense.

"Seriously detectives?" Diane asked. "I thought that it had been decided that I had nothing to do with Maxwell Carter's murder."

"The evidence leans toward you not being physically able to commit the murder," Detective Thom said. "There is still probable cause to believe that you may be involved or, based on your assertion that someone was in here without your knowledge, something of interest to the case in your possession."

Diane sighed and requested Charles Godfrey's presence for the search. The detectives reluctantly agreed to wait a short time until the lawyer arrived. Diane took her cell phone from her purse and called Charles, explaining that the police were in her chalet with a search warrant. Diane was surprised when Charles joined Diane and the detectives only fifteen minutes later. When he arrived, the detectives gave him the warrant. He reviewed it and nodded.

"Everything appears to be in order, and it appears you were able to convince a judge to sign," he said. "Although I dare say the probable cause for this search is thin by any standards, but that can be dealt with down the line should it become necessary."

"Right, then we will get started," Detective Thom said. "If you will please stand to the side and let us do our job."

The detectives put on latex gloves and began their search, while Charles led Diane to a small sitting area for a private discussion.

"Well, I suspect this must be becoming very stressful," he asked Diane. "Are you okay?"

"I believe so," she said. "I'm just getting extremely frustrated with the situation, but I do so appreciate you coming so very quickly. It's like you were just around the corner!"

"Of course," he said. "It was the right decision to call me. We do not want these detectives, or anyone with the police station for that matter, to make assumptions should anything be found. It is important that you call me anytime there is a chance of new evidence."

"I agree," Diane said. "And I absolutely will." She felt a slight sense of guilt at not being able to tell him about what she had already discovered.

Detectives Donnelly and Thom spent almost two hours searching Diane's chalet, going through every cabinet, cushion, corner, computer file and piece of clothing she had. She found it quite unnerving and even a little embarrassing at times, but was relieved when nothing of interest to the case was located. Well, nothing else, she thought. She expected the memory card was still safely under the rock outside and hoped that the detectives found no reason to search in the garden.

"I think we are done in here," Detective Thom said. "Do not plan on leaving, just yet, however. Depending on the evidence we are continuing to collect in this case, the forensics team may need to come back and do some testing on the mysterious opening window."

Diane was unsure if Detective Thom was being sarcastic about the window, but decided at this point she did not care. She was just ready for everyone to leave her be, mainly so she could retrieve the memory card and review what might be on it privately.

"I plan to stay a few more days, but I cannot stay here indefinitely for you to keep questioning me about something I had nothing to do with," Diane said, although she did plan on staying to continue her own investigation into what occurred.

Diane thanked Charles, who left with the detectives. She looked out of her window and watched Charles speaking with the detectives as they stood next to the garden area. Her eyes lingered on the rock until movement caused her to look back to Charles and the detectives. Just as she decided to go outside to find out what they were discussing, it appeared their conversation was over. They all walked toward their cars, got in and left. Diane made a mental note to ask Charles what he had been discussing with the detectives the next time she saw him.

Chapter 14

After waiting for about thirty minutes, Diane looked outside and saw no sign of the detectives or Charles. She walked outside to the garden area and continued to look around for any sign of unwanted visitors. Satisfied that no one was watching, she picked up the rock, quickly grabbed the paper towel holding the memory card and put it into her pocket. She then put the rock back, making sure it was in exactly the same spot, and hurried inside. Diane realized she was lucky that while they had searched her electronic devices, they had not taken them into evidence for further searches. She was extremely eager to see what was on the memory card but also nervous about what traces might be left behind on her computer. Deciding that what was on the memory card was proof of her lack of involvement in the crime and considering the detective had not technically asked her if she knew where the memory card was after she found it, Diane powered up her laptop and inserted the card.

It turned out Angela's concerns over the pictures were somewhat warranted. There were several black and white photos of Angela and Maxwell in various stages of undress, although nothing completely nude. Diane thought the photos appeared to show a loving couple that was comfortable with each other. Angela even had a small tattoo on her upper arm that read "Angela &

Maxwell Forever." The next photos on the card seemed to contradict the tattoo as they pictured Maxwell with another woman. These photos also showed various stages of undress. Diane did not recognize her but wondered if this was meant to be art or something more. The final pictures on the card were of great interest to Diane, and certainly would be of great interest to the police. A series of photos showed the umbrella rolling across the beach, and Diane grabbing it right before it was lifted out to sea.

Diane now understood why Maxwell was so upset with her when she grabbed the umbrella. He was in the midst of an artistic photo shoot, and she had mistakenly ruined it. Diane recalled the photos she had seen in the exhibit at the local art center, and the images of the umbrella she saw on the memory card fit the photographer's style. Still, she thought, he could have simply explained what he was trying to do instead of being so rude. Diane continued looking through the pictures that were taken after the one of her grabbing the umbrella. It looked like Maxwell had tried to redo the shoot. There were a number of pictures of the umbrella, followed by pictures of the sky and then the sand. The next picture on the card really caught Diane's attention when she noticed a person's leg.

It had to be the killer's leg, she thought, and it was certainly a leg that could be easily identified. Although slightly out of focus, there was some type of ugly mark or scar on the leg. A burn mark perhaps, Diane thought. The more she looked at it, the more she felt something familiar about the mark on the leg.

"Judith Moseley," she said to herself, staring at the picture. The picture of the leg was the last one of the memory card, so it had to be the person who killed Maxwell Carter. Diane sat down on her chair, relieved that there was now some evidence of the killer as well as concerned that someone had put the memory card in her room. She could think of no explanation as to who could have known when she would not be around or who could have had such easy access. Diane was sure that if she told the detectives about what she had found, they likely would come back and check for fingerprints on the window. Drat, she thought, how was she going to tell the detectives about this? In hindsight, perhaps it would have been better for them to find the card during their search as the pictures clearly showed she did not attack or otherwise harm Maxwell Carter. She would have to find a way to get it to the police. Diane decided that a phone call to Charles Godfrey was now warranted. She fished her cell phone from her bag and dialed his number.

"Hello?" he answered.

"Charles, this is Diane Dimbleby," she said. "I'm sorry to bother you so soon after you've gone, but I've gotten somewhat of a sticky wicket situation."

"No bother at all, Diane," he said. "Are those detectives back again?"

"No," she said. "At least, not yet. I actually came across a memory card in my couch after everyone left."

"I see," Charles said. "Stay right there, and do not call anyone else. I will be over shortly to retrieve it from you."

Charles' offer seemed strange to Diane. Perhaps he was just trying to protect her, but why would he want to come and get the memory card from her? She had expected him to make arrangements to meet her at the police station.

"Thank you, Charles, but there is no need for you to come get it," she said. "I prefer to take it to Detective Donnelly and Detective Thom myself. I just thought you would like to know what had happened. I would be grateful if you would meet me at the station."

Charles was silent for a few seconds before replying. "Sure, sure," he said. "Don't go just yet. I have some time-sensitive tasks I need to get done."

"Of course," she said. "I'll have lunch here and then head that way in about an hour."

"Good then," he said, hanging up the phone rather abruptly.

Chapter 15

Diane put the card in a small pocket in the front of her bag and went to the kitchenette to make a sandwich. She used some ham that she had picked up from the market the day before and added a bag of crisps. As she ate, she replayed the conversation with Charles in her mind. He had seemed very eager to take the memory card from her, but perhaps that was normal in this situation. She finished her lunch, looked at her watch and noted that almost 45 minutes had passed since her conversation with Charles. She took the next 15 minutes to clean up her lunch mess, freshen her face and gather her things. She double checked her purse pocket for the memory card and walked to her car. As she began to back out of the small parking area, a car pulled quickly up behind her. She looked in her rearview mirror and noticed it was Charles' silver Mercedes Benz.

"Well, I told him I would meet him at the station in an hour," she said, annoyed. She started to open her car door to remind him that they were supposed to meet at the police station and saw him holding a small pistol out in front of him. Diane pushed the locks on her hire car as Charles walked to the driver's side window, pointing the gun at her. She did not have time to get her window up before he started threatening her.

"Open the door and get out of the car, Diane," he said. "Open it now. I have no want or need to hurt you, but I will if I have to."

"Oh gracious, really?" Diane said. His grandstanding and gun-waving was just too much.

Although terrified of what he might do, she turned her head away from him. If she opened the door, he surely would grab her purse and anything else that might hold the memory card.

"I am tired of waiting," he said, still standing several feet away. "Open this car door now, or I will open it for you."

Diane leaned forward, her head under the steering wheel. She quickly pulled the memory card out of the front pocket of her purse and slipped it into her bra. Not wanting to face Charles, she kept her head down until she felt him right next to the car. Her body began to shake with fear as she heard his heavy breathing.

"I warned you Diane," he said. Charles was right next to her car door and pointed his gun through the window. Diane closed her eyes, leaning her body as far forward as possible. As she reached out her hand, she felt something cylindrical. Her fingers closed around the can of lubricant spray she had bought the previous day. Counting quickly to herself, Diane sprung up with the lubricant in her hand and sprayed Charles directly into the eyes.

Charles screamed in agony, backing away from the car and falling onto the ground. The sudden blindness, or perhaps just the jolt of the fall, caused Charles to fire the gun. Diane ducked down into the car again before realizing that Charles had fired the gun straight up into the air. She started to turn the key in the ignition and try to force her way out of the corner Charles had put her in with his car when she heard police sirens. Charles continued to lay on the ground, whimpering in pain. The sirens continued to get closer, and Diane realized they were headed toward them.

"Thank goodness," she said.

Detectives Donnelly and Thom, accompanied by two police officers in a standard cruiser, pulled up behind Charles' silver Mercedes Benz. Diane then found herself surrounded by more people pointing guns in her direction. This was becoming a problem, she decided, and yearned for her home in Apple Mews.

"Freeze!" Detective Donnelly yelled at Charles as he continued to moan and move around.

"My eyes! Oh, my eyes!" he cried. "I think she blinded me."

"Settle down Godfrey," Detective Thom said. "And put your hands behind your back."

Two of the police officers accompanying the detectives surrounded the grumbling lawyer and pulled him to his feet. Detective Donnelly grabbed his arms, pulled them behind his back and handcuffed him. Detective Thom escorted Godfrey back to one of the police cruisers, putting his hand behind his head while helping him into the back seat.

"I'm sure you know this by heart, but let's go over it anyway," Detective Thom said. "You do not have to say anything, but it may harm your defense if you do not mention when questioned something which you later rely on in court. Anything you say may be given in evidence. Do you have any questions about what I have told you?"

Godfrey gave the detective a steely look, grumbled under his breath and shook his head slightly.

"I will take that as a no," the detective said. "Take him back to the station and start processing him."

While Detective Thom and the officers dealt with Godfrey, Detective Donnelly turned her attention to Diane who had gotten out of the car and was watching the situation with Charles Godfrey unfold. The detective started walking to the car, and Diane slowly raised her hands behind her head. She fully expected to also be placed into handcuffs.

"I found the memory card, detective," she said. "I believe that is what Mr. Godfrey was after, although I am not sure why. I managed to slip it into my bra."

Detective Donnelly stifled a small chuckle and smiled warmly at Diane. "No need for that, Diane," she said. "You can put your hands down, and I'll take that card."

Diane lowered her hands, turned slightly from Detective Donnelly and reached into the top of her bra. She pulled out the memory card and handed it over. Detective Donnelly pulled out a plastic bag and took the memory card without touching it.

"You never know whose prints might be on it," the detective said. "Besides yours, of course. Why don't we go inside and have a cup of tea to calm down a bit. Then we will head back to the station and straighten the rest of this out."

Diane agreed, and the detectives followed her back into the chalet.

Chapter 16

After finishing their tea, Detectives Donnelly and Thom drove Diane to the police station. Instead of returning to an interrogation room, she was taken to the superintendent's office. Superintendent Darren McDougall stood to greet Diane as she was led into his office by an assistant. Diane took a seat across from Superintendent McDougall who sat behind a massive wooden desk littered with files, empty coffee cups and what Diane assumed were pictures of his family. There were several awards, commendations and framed newspaper articles adorning the walls of his office.

"Ms. Dimbleby, thank you for coming," McDougall said. Diane started to say that there was no need to thank her because her visits to the police station had not exactly been completely voluntary of late but thought better of it. "Please call me Diane," she said instead.

"Diane, we have had the opportunity to interview Charles Godfrey, as well as the gallery owner, and have learned some information that may be of interest to you," he said. "It certainly is of interest to us."

The superintendent explained that Maxwell Carter had made quite a name for himself as a photographer. A handful of wealthy socialites had taken notice of his work, purchasing whole exhibits at a time. His name then began to spread, and he received a number of offers to showcase his work, the last of which was at a local art gallery.

"Yes, I saw his exhibit," Diane said. "It was, well, um, eclectic."

"I suppose that is a good description of an exhibit that goes from a watering can to scantily dressed women," the superintendent said.

He went on to explain that the photographer was very interested in the female form, as evidenced by several exhibits. He often included nudes, usually ex-girlfriends. Diane was reminded of the photos she had seen of Detective Donnelly at the exhibit.

"Did you know that Hazel Donnelly modeled for Maxwell Carter?" she asked. "There are pictures of her in the exhibit at the art center. She appears very young, but I am certain it is her."

The superintendent nodded. "Detective Donnelly has been very open about this," he said. "When she first came onto the force, she disclosed this information. She is obviously not proud of what occurred, but as you have pointed out, the pictures were taken when she was young."

"Why didn't you take her off of the case when it was discovered who the victim was?" Diane said. "I mean, considering her possible relationship with him."

"There was no reason to take her off the case because there was no relationship," he said. "At least, not in the way you think. There was no personal relationship between Hazel Donnelly and Maxwell Carter."

"How can you be sure of that?" she asked.

"I can be sure of that because I trust my detective," he said. "She was very clear that it was an afternoon of modeling work several years ago, and there is no evidence to contradict that."

The superintendent explained that the erotic photos were big sellers for Maxwell and the galleries that showcased his work. In fact, the local gallery owner had encouraged him to shoot and include more nude photos.

"Apparently the commission on the sales of the nude photos was substantial, and the gallery owner wanted his piece of the pie," McDougall said. "As soon as one of the nudes sold, he was pressuring Mr. Carter for more."

Diane recalled her interaction with the gallery owner, and his dismissal of her to focus on the patrons he believed were wealthy enough to make large purchases. She could see based on his actions that he was more interested in money than art.

"So Mr. Carter continued to enlist women for his exhibits, and his reputation of such continued to grow," McDougall said. "Everything was running along smoothly for him until he started dating Angela Godfrey."

"Godfrey?" Diane said, suddenly realizing the connection. "I take it Angela Godfrey is Charles Godfrey's daughter."

"Correct," he said. "I understand you had an interaction with her."

"I suppose an interaction is one way to put it," she said. "I also take it that Charles did not approve of his daughter's selection of suitor."

"Correct again," he said. "When Charles Godfrey learned his daughter was dating such a "cad"—his words, not mine—he became annoyed at first, and then when his daughter did not end things, angry. Being a highly respected and powerful lawyer in this area, he did not want his daughter or his name associated with such things."

After he had discovered the relationship, Charles Godfrey demanded his daughter end the relationship. Angela, being her father's daughter, flat-out refused. She had decided that she was in love with Maxwell and had no intention of acquiescing to her father.

"Charles did not hide his disdain for either Maxwell Carter or the relationship with his daughter," McDougall said. "Mr. Carter was very well aware of how his girlfriend's father felt."

With this information, Diane thought of another reason why Maxwell would have been so insolent to her at the beach. He may have thought she was trying to sabotage his work on Charles' behalf. After all, they had spent a fair amount of time together talking at the wedding. It was possible that Maxwell either saw the two together at some point or was made aware of the connection.

"Mr. Godfrey has continued to deny he committed the murder," McDougall said. "But I expect we will have a confession soon enough."

"I wouldn't be so sure," Diane said.

"Detectives Donnelly and Thom are on it," he said. "They will get the confession."

"No, I mean they shouldn't bother," she said.

"What?" he asked. "Why ever not?"

"Charles Godfrey did not kill Maxwell Carter," Diane said.

"What makes you say that?" the superintendent asked. "Based on the evidence and the way he pulled a gun on you, he is certainly on the top of the suspect list. And there is not denying he had a motive."

"The reasoning behind his actions are not those of a murderer," she said.

"Well, then whose actions are?" he asked.

"Do you have the photos that were on the memory card?" she asked.

"Yes, I have copies of them here," he said.

Superintendent McDougall pulled the photographs from a folder on his desk and laid them out in front of him. Diane rose and stood next to him behind the desk.

"May I?" she asked, reaching for the photos.

"Be my guest," he said.

Diane picked through the photos until she found one of Angela that displayed her arm and the photo that showed the killer's leg. She placed the two next to one another and turned toward McDougall.

"Here is a picture of Angela's arm," she began. "You can clearly see it is her, and that she has a tattoo on her arm declaring her love for Matthew."

"Yes," the superintendent said. "That only bolster's the theory that Charles Godfrey is the killer. I am quite sure he was as unhappy with the tattoo as he was with the relationship. Perhaps even more so."

"I have no doubt, but I dare say he was not the only one," she said, picking up the picture of the leg. "As it appears to be the very last one taken, this photo likely shows the killer's leg."

"That is a fair assumption," McDougall said.

"The leg in this picture has a scarred, ugly mark on it," Diane said. "It looks almost like a burn, but it is not. This mark was left when a tattoo was removed. I am quite certain it was another tattoo regarding Angela and Maxwell's relationship, and the leg in the photo belongs to Angela."

"How could you possibly know any of that?" McDougall asked.

Diane explained that the mark on the leg had reminded her of a woman back in Apple Mews. The woman, Judith Moseley, had been somewhat naïve in her youth about a man she had met. Judith was sure that the man was her soul mate, and she had a similar tattoo placed on her leg thinking they would spend their lives together. A few months after her tribute to the relationship, Judith learned that the man was married and had no intention of carrying on the tryst with her.

"Judith could not bear to look at the tattoo every day, so she decided to have it removed," Diane said. "She found a dermatologist and endured laser removal. The process left a very similar type of scar on her leg."

"Why would Angela have the tattoo removed?" he said.

"That's why," Diane said, pointing to the pictures of the other woman on the memory card. "She must have discovered that Maxwell was seeing another woman and realized that their relationship was just like all of his other relationships. I suspect Angela has already scheduled the appointment to remove the tattoo on her arm."

"It is possible that Charles found all of this out as well and was trying to protect his daughter," McDougall said.

"Oh, it is more than possible," Diane said. "Remember, I said that the reasoning behind his actions were not those of a murderer. I believe the reasoning is exactly what you have stated—a father wanting to protect his daughter. I do believe that is why Charles was so interested in helping me, turning up almost instantly whenever called."

"He did point a gun at you," McDougall said.

"Yes, but he did not fire the gun at me," she retorted. "And he certainly had the opportunity to. No, I think that the person capable of murder here is the woman scorned."

Diane theorized that Angela likely found out about the other girl several weeks earlier. "After all," she said. "It takes more than a few days to remove a tattoo. I expect she had that done immediately and continued plotting her revenge."

"If he was done with her, how did she know about his trip to the beach?" he asked.

"I don't think he was quite done with her, at least not yet, and she certainly was not done with him," Diane said. "She would not have let on that she knew about the other woman, or that would have ruined her opportunity for retribution. Angela was biding her time and must have followed him daily waiting for her opportunity to pounce."

Diane decided that Angela must have been watching Maxwell set up his photo shoot on the beach the day of the murder. When Diane and Maxwell appeared to be arguing after she had picked up his umbrella, Angela knew that it was the perfect opportunity to take care of her cheating boyfriend while pointing the evidence to someone else.

"As soon as I touched that umbrella, I suspect everything fell into place in Angela's mind," Diane said. "The terse conversation between us only helped her."

"How do you think she was able to pull this off without you seeing her?" McDougall asked.

"I went about my business immediately after speaking with him," she said. "And there was no one around on the beach when I left. I suspect that as soon as I was well out of sight, Angela approached Maxwell. She could have even surprised him while he was setting up his photo shoot again. In fact, I am sure based on the series of photos that this is exactly what happened."

Diane went over the photos again with Superintendent McDougall, pointing out the sequence of photos that ended abruptly with the picture of the leg. Angela interrupted the photo shoot, likely causing an argument. After all, this was at least the second time Maxwell had attempted the same thing and was interrupted.

"Perhaps she grabbed the camera from him when she approached him, and it went off," Diane said. "That would explain the angle of the leg shot and would have given her the opportunity to remove the memory card from the camera."

Once the memory card was removed, the argument likely escalated further. Angela, enraged by the other woman, grabbed the umbrella and drove it into Maxwell's chest. With no one else on the beach, she wiped her prints off of the umbrella and the camera and hurried away.

"Then how did she know who you were, and where to plant the memory card?" he asked.

"Angela had been following Maxwell for days, probably even weeks," Diane said. "My chalet is right near the beach. She must have watched me leave."

Diane believed that after Angela saw Diane get on the tour bus, she went to the window of the chalet she saw Diane coming from, climbed through and hid the memory card under a couch cushion. She also thought it unlikely that any fingerprints would be found, as Angela had been extremely careful about removing her prints from the crime scene and leaving only Diane's.

"She ultimately realized later that while the memory card could implicate me in the murder, there was also a possibility it could implicate her," she said. "I expect she was working on pure adrenaline when she rushed to place it in my possession and did not consider the possibility that it could implicate her as well."

Once reality set in for Angela, she was desperate to get the memory card back to make sure that there were no photos on it that would point to her as a suspect. Angela expected there to be photos from the beach shoot, but it did not occur to her until after she planted the memory card at Diane's that there could be other photos as well. Despite the amount of time Angela and Maxwell had spent together, she did not know his work habits—specifically when he cleaned off his memory card.

"When Angela approached me, she gave me quite a convincing sob story about why she was looking for the photos," Diane said. "It was clear she was desperate to get her hands on the memory card. And when I did not help, she called in her father."

"So you don't think Charles told her anything about the murder or you before then?" McDougall asked.

"Not until she had to get the memory card," she said. "I think it was just coincidence that I had met Charles at the wedding and called him when I realized I was suspected of something. He learned later from his daughter what had occurred when she could not get the memory card back. After he had tried and failed to get access to the memory card as my lawyer, he became desperate and confronted me."

Superintendent McDougall nodded slightly and agreed to look into the theory. He said he would have Detective Donnelly contact dermatologists in the area who provided laser tattoo removal, and Detective Thom would be tasked with coordinating with the forensics team to see if Angela could have committed the crime.

"We will also gather fingerprints from your window," he said. "Someone obviously broke in to leave the memory card. They may have been wearing gloves, but it certainly is worth a look."

"Thank you Superintendent McDougall, but I doubt that Angela would have left any prints behind," she said. "Why don't you just ask her to show you her leg to see if the mark is there?"

"If what you are saying is true, we need to get some more probable cause to bring Angela in," he said. "We don't want to show our hand making her decide to disappear."

Diane understood. Angela Godfrey had lived a charmed, wealthy life thanks to her father. There surely was enough money available to her if she chose to run.

"I'm sorry you were dragged into this," McDougall said. "I hope you understand we can only go where the evidence leads and, for a short time at least, the evidence was leading to you."

"I suppose so," she said. "I take it I am free to go back to Apple Mews now."

"Absolutely," he said. "After all you've said and been through, I thought you might want to stay long enough to see this sorted out."

"I have no doubt you will get things sorted out by tomorrow," Diane said. "Regardless, that will be when I leave."

Chapter 17

Detective Donnelly took Diane back to her chalet and walked her in. She took out a small fingerprint kit and dusted the window sill, latch and the panes surrounding the latch. She pulled out what appeared to be clear tape and lifted a number of prints.

"I expect some, or all of these will belong to you," Detective Donnelly said.

"I imagine so," Diane said. "It will be like umbrella déjà vu."

Detective Donnelly let out a small laugh, and Diane offered her a warm smile in return. "I did want to thank you for showing up in the nick of time," Diane said. "I still do not think Charles would have harmed me, but it does not mean that I was not scared."

"It's my job," she said. "I do hope that your time in Devon was not all bad."

This reminded Diane of her nephew's wedding, which seemed so long ago. She had been happy to be there and enjoyed seeing her family. Oh drat, she thought. She had told her brother that she would come to dinner before leaving town. He still had no idea what had happened.

"Thank you Hazel," Diane said, jumping to her feet and escorting the detective to the door. "I'm afraid I must say a quick goodbye. I owe my brother a visit before I leave, and I fully intend on leaving tomorrow."

Detective Donnelly left, and Diane called her brother. She filled him in on what had occurred over the past few days. Although annoyed she had not told him earlier, Martin knew his sister would not have wanted to worry anyone. She made plans to come by in the morning for brunch before heading back to Apple Mews. Diane then spent the next few hours cleaning up her chalet, packing her clothes and getting ready to leave the next morning. She gathered any leftover food and prepared it to take to the food pantry on her way to Martin's house the following morning. It was close to 9 p.m. when the gravity of the last few days finally caught up with her. Although she had planned to spend a little time writing, her eyes and body became too heavy, and she decided to turn in.

Chapter 18

After waking up a little after dawn, Diane was eager to get back to Apples Mews. She popped out of bed, got ready and finished loading her hire car. She left a thank you note and the key to the chalet before heading to her brother's house. When she arrived, Martin and Suzanne were sitting on the front porch drinking coffee and reading the paper.

"Well, there she is," Martin said, walking to Diane and offering her a hug.

"Good morning," Diane said.

"I cannot believe you kept us in the dark about this," Suzanne said, holding up the morning paper.

On the front page was a picture of Maxwell Carter, next to pictures of Angela and Charles Godfrey. The headline read PROMINENT LAWYER'S DAUGHTER ARRESTED FOR THE MURDER OF MAXWELL CARTER.

"They did work fast," Diane mumbled under her breath.

"What was that?" Suzanne asked.

"Oh nothing," Diane said.

"Now explain to me again what happened," Martin said. "And don't leave anything out."

"I will," she said. "Let's have something to eat, and I will tell you the whole sordid tale."

They all sat down to brunch, and Diane relived the past few days in detail. When they were done, Martin walked Diane to her hire car, and she asked him if she could have the copy of the paper.

"Of course," he said. "Although I'm not sure why you would want it."

"Let's just say it will be a reminder of how much I love Apple Mews," she said before getting in the car and pointing it toward home.

Get Your Free Copy of "Murder at the Inn".

Don't forget to grab your free copy of Penelope Sotheby's first novella *Murder At The Inn* while you still can.

Go to http://fantasticfiction.info/murder-at-the-inn/ to find out more.

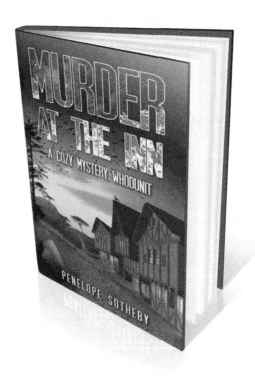

Other Books by This Author

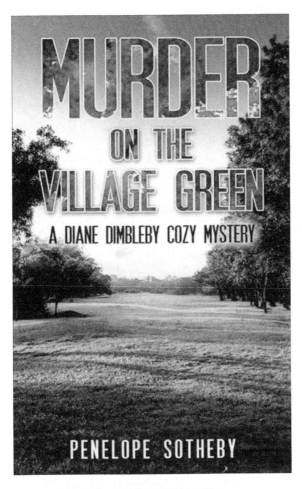

Murder on the Village Green

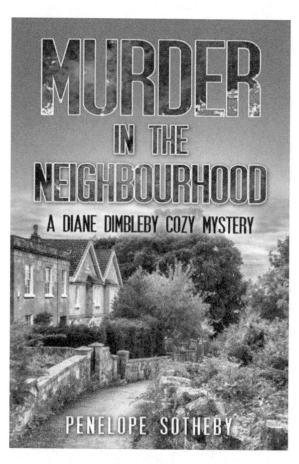

Murder in the Neighbourhood

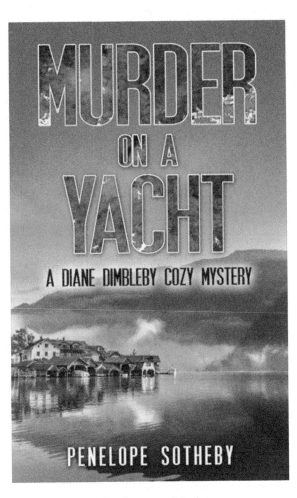

Murder on a Yacht

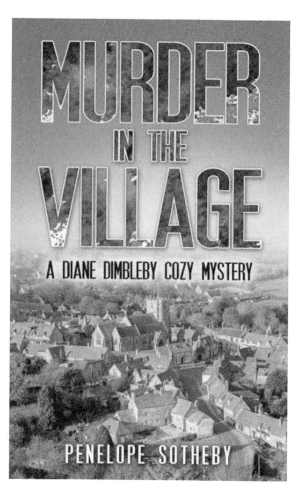

Murder in the Village

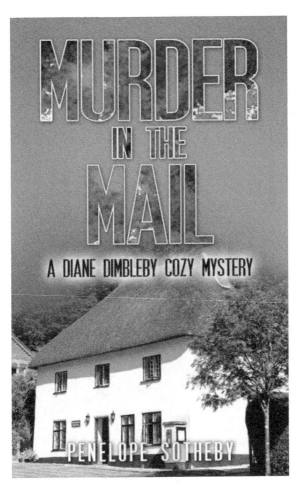

Murder in the Mail

Murder in the Development

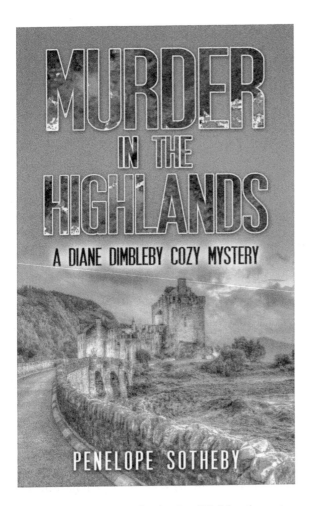

Murder in the Highlands

About The Author

For many, the thought of childhood conjures images of hopscotch games in quiet neighbourhoods, and sticky visits to the local sweet shop. For Penelope Sotheby, childhood meant bathing in Bermuda, jiving in Jamaica and exploring a string of strange and exotic British territories with her nomadic family. New friends would come and go, but her constant companion was an old, battered collection of Agatha Christie novels that filled her hours with intrigue and wonder.

Penelope would go on to read every single one of Christie's sixty-six novels—multiple times—and so was born a love of suspense than can be found in Sotheby's own works today.

In 2011 the author debuted with *"Murder at the Inn"*, a whodunit novella set on Graham Island off the West Coast of Canada. After receiving positive acclaim, Sotheby went on to write the series *"Murder in Paradise"*; five novels following the antics of a wedding planner navigating nuptials (and crime scenes) in the tropical locations of Sotheby's formative years.

An avid gardener, proud mother, and passionate host of Murder Mystery weekends, Sotheby can often be found at her large oak table, gleefully plotting the demise of her friends, tricky twists and grand reveals.

Fantastic Fiction

Fantastic Fiction publishes short reads that feature stories in a series of five or more books. Specializing in genres such as Mystery, Thriller, Fantasy and Sci Fi, our novels are exciting and put our readers at the edge of their seats.

Each of our novellas range around 20,000 words each and are perfect for short afternoon reads. Most of the stories published through Fantastic Fiction are escapist fiction and allow readers to indulge in their imagination through well written, powerful and descriptive stories.

Why Fiction?

At Fantastic Fiction, we believe that life doesn't get much better than kicking back and reading a gripping piece of fiction. We are passionate about supporting independent writers and believe that the world should have access to this incredible works of fiction. Through our store we provide a diverse range of fiction that is sure to satisfy.

www.fantasticfiction.info

Made in the USA
Columbia, SC
16 July 2024